THE
GLASS
MERMAID

by SUSAN CLYMER

Illustrated by PAMELA JOHNSON

SCHOLASTIC INC.
NEW YORK • TORONTO • LONDON • AUCKLAND • SYDNEY

To young writers everywhere.

ISBN 0-590-32839-5

Text copyright © 1986 by Susan Clymer.
Illustrations copyright © 1986 by Scholastic Books, Inc.
All rights reserved. Published by Scholastic Inc.
Art direction by Diana Hrisinko./Text design by Sarah McElwain.

12 11 10 9 8 7 6 5 4 3 2 1   10   6 7 8 9/8 0 1/9

✄ Christmas Eve ✄

BECCA sat straight up in bed. She had done it! She was awake in the middle of the night on Christmas Eve. Becca pulled on tennis shoes and a heavy sweater over her pajamas. Then she peered into the dark, silent hallway. Her mother and her sister Adelle must be sound asleep. Becca tiptoed down the hallway. The bright hands on the hall clock said ten to twelve. Midnight!

At the turn of the stairs, Becca stretched onto her toes and looked out her favorite window. Flakes of snow drifted down through the night sky. Maybe tomorrow would be a white Christmas!

The trees already had a little dusting of white on their branches. Becca shivered happily. Anything could happen on a night like this.

Becca hurried down the stairs. She wanted to look at the new presents under the tree all alone. She wanted to poke them and shake them and dream about what they might be inside. There must be new ones for her. When Becca had gone to bed, her sister Adelle had still had two more presents than she under the tree. Becca stopped at the bottom of the stairs. The Christmas tree looked ghostly. Light from the streetlight outside shone on the ornaments and tinsel. Suddenly something moved on the side of the tree. Her favorite ornament was swaying in the ghostly light. Becca rushed forward. She crouched down and caught the glass mermaid just as it slipped off its holder.

"Thank goodness!" a small voice said.

Becca looked in amazement at the mermaid in her hand. "Did you say something?"

"No, I did," a voice replied above her. Becca saw a boy standing in the Christmas tree. He couldn't be any more than six inches tall. The boy balanced on a tiny limb.

"Guess I'm too heavy," the boy said. "The branch got to swaying and the mermaid —"

"Who are you?" Becca interrupted.

The boy gazed at her. "You don't look dangerous. Even if you are big as a mountain. Jingle is my name. I make the finest bells in all of Seatown." He took off his cap and bowed low. Little bells on his wrists and around his neck jingled. He bowed so low that he lost his balance and tumbled off the swaying limb.

Becca gasped. She cradled the mermaid ornament in one hand and put her other hand out to catch him. The boy turned a perfect somersault in the air. Then he landed on the edge of her palm with both feet.

"Ouch!" Becca cried. The boy rolled away. He was graceful even when he fell, just like her sister Adelle. Becca put her stinging palm under her arm and leaped silently around the room.

She heard a chorus of giggles.

Becca dropped to her knees in front of the boy and saw another little person. The two of them stood in a path of light. "I may be crazy, but I think you're real!"

The giggling stopped. "Real as a whale's tail!" the other person said. Becca could tell it was a woman from the voice.

Both tiny people wore trousers, wide-bottomed

shirts that came almost to their knees, and flat caps. Jingle had on a green shirt and brown trousers. The woman wore all red. She stood with one thumb stuck in the red waistband of her pants. Her cap sat sideways on her head, and a bundle was tied to her back. The tiny woman had rolled her red sleeves up to her elbows. Becca liked red. "My name is Becca. What's yours?" she asked.

"Sander. I build boats. Then I sand them until they gleam. You see, in Seatown we name ourselves after what we do best. I sand boats."

Jingle leaped for both ends of a piece of tinsel and swung on it. His bells jingled. He even had bells around his ankles.

"Where is Seatown?" Becca asked. The palms of her hands and the bottoms of her feet tingled. Imagine! She was talking to tiny people in her living room in the middle of Christmas Eve.

The tinsel Jingle was swinging on broke, but he landed on his feet. His bells rang even louder. "Not far," he said.

"But how did you get here?" Becca demanded.

Sander picked a pine needle as long as her arm. She stuck it into her back pocket, and the needle plumed over her head like a peacock tail. "Through your Christmas tree."

"Through what?!" This was too much. Becca didn't believe her.

"We need a mermaid," Sander said.

Jingle waved his arm so excitedly that the bells around his wrist jingled. Becca wished the constant tinkling would stop, at least for a second. "We have heard stories that you big people hang tiny angels, and snowmen, and even mermaids from your trees!" Jingle exclaimed.

"That's why you're here?" Becca clutched the gold and red ornament against her chest. Her grandfather had given the mermaid to her when she was three years old. "You want to take my mermaid!" Becca jumped to her feet. She tripped over her shoelaces and almost stumbled over the two tiny people in front of her.

Sander backed away and disappeared around the trunk of the Christmas tree. Jingle followed, only he ran on his hands instead of his feet.

They were going! She would never see them again. "Wait!" Becca exclaimed. "Wait for me! I won't hurt you." Becca had to lay down on her belly and oozle around to the back of the tree. "Why do you want my mermaid?" Becca bumped into a present and pushed it aside.

Sander and Jingle stood beside a tiny, lit doorway in the trunk of the tree. Amazed, Becca put down the mermaid. What was a doorway doing in her Christmas tree? She reached out to touch the miniature doorknob. Instantly, the little people, the tree, and the floor swirled around her. Becca closed her eyes to keep from getting dizzy.

When she opened her eyes again, Becca looked up into the branches of a giant tree. Sander was leaning over her. The woman looked huge. "Did you grow?" Becca asked.

"No!" Sander exclaimed. "You shrank!"

"You touched the doorknob." Jingle rocked back and forth, setting off all his little bells. "Now you're the same size as us!"

Becca stumbled to her feet. Right beside her lay the mermaid ornament. Usually it wasn't any longer than one of her hands. Now it was almost as big as her whole body. Becca could barely swallow. Her voice came out like a squeak. "What will I do? I can't stay like this."

Sander and Jingle looked at each other. "Have to take her to The Captain," Sander whispered. "The Captain might be able to help her get big again."

"The Captain?" Becca asked.

Jingle swung around to face Becca. "The Captain is a sorceress. She lives on a ship outside

Seatown. She uses magic. *Evil* magic." He sounded terrified. "She sends storms to make ships sink. She calls dolphins and mermaids to her and then she *eats* them."

Becca's mouth went dry and her knees felt wobbly.

"The Captain turns people into animals and rocks!" Jingle cried. "She . . ."

Sander grabbed Jingle's shoulders to make him stop. "*Sometimes* The Captain grants us favors, Becca. She used to be one of us when she was a little girl."

"She only grants us favors so the children will be tempted by her," Jingle exclaimed. "The sorceress is a horrible trickster!"

"But this is silly," Becca said bravely. "I don't believe in sorceresses."

"You will soon," Sander replied.

✂

⟩⟨ *Curious as a Catfish* ⟩⟨

SANDER and Jingle picked up the mermaid ornament and walked through the doorway into the Christmas tree. "Where are you going with my mermaid?" Becca cried. Her voice echoed after them in the tunnel.

"To see The Captain," Sander replied gently. "Come on, girl. Come into our world."

Becca hesitated at the doorway. She had to go with them. There wasn't any other way to get big again. Becca looked up in the direction of her mother's bedroom. She wished she could leave a note, but the pencil would be bigger than she was. Besides, what would she say. . . .

> Dear Mother,
>   Gone into the Christmas tree to see a sorceress.
>
>   Love,
>   Becca

Her mother wouldn't believe her anyway.

Jingle twisted his head to look back at her, making the bells on his cap ring. All that jingling would drive her crazy! Jingle carried the mermaid's tail. "Don't you want to get big again, Purple Flower?" he asked.

"Purple Flower?!" Becca exclaimed.

Jingle grinned. "Your pants have purple flowers on them. When you were big, they were *giant* purple flowers. It's a good nickname."

Becca looked down at her pajamas. "They are pink." At least they were supposed to be pink flowers, but that was before the pajamas had gotten washed with her sister's bright purple dancing tights.

Becca took a deep breath and followed Sander and Jingle into the Christmas tree. They walked down a flight of dimly lit stairs, sticky with sap.

Becca felt as if her shoes were almost glued to the stairs with wads of bubble gum.

Yet in front of her, Jingle bounced off each tiny step on his toes as if at any moment he might leap into the air. His bells jingled on every bounce. He was graceful even while carrying the mermaid.

Just like Adelle, Becca thought. Her sister Adelle always danced everywhere, graceful as a fairy. She was only a year older than Becca, yet she danced with the city ballet troupe. She'd even acted in a show.

Becca was more like an awkward, clumsy elephant. Sometimes she felt as if she didn't even belong in the same family with someone like Adelle. Yet right now, Becca knew she would give anything to see her sister.

"What if I'm trapped in a little body forever?" she moaned.

No one answered. Becca twisted her head from side to side. Then she moved her shoulders. Her body didn't feel different. She was just little, little enough to be walking inside a Christmas tree trunk. The stairs curved down and down and down. Finally, Becca saw the end of the stairway. A silver star hung from the roof. It glistened and sparkled in the moonlight.

Jingle reached up to touch the star with one

hand. "This is the finest of my bells," Jingle said. A soft ringing pierced the air. The sound was so beautiful that Becca gasped. She reached up to touch the bell and bumped into Jingle.

"Sorry," she muttered, but Becca didn't really feel sorry. She hated being clumsy.

Jingle hopped from foot to foot. Couldn't he ever stand still? Everything he did reminded her of Adelle. Jingle touched his bell again. "Shall I leave it here, Purple Flower?" he said softly. "For your journey home?"

Home. Becca swirled back to look at the stairs. "Sander! Sander! Is this tunnel always open?"

Sander sighed. "Curious as a catfish, you are. The passageway is open one night a year, on your Christmas Eve. 'Tis a magical night."

"Then I have to get home tonight? Or I won't get home for a whole year?" Becca felt her stomach slip all the way down to her toes.

Sander nodded solemnly. "The passageway closes at dawn." The woman stepped out into the moonlight, tugging Jingle along with her. "Slow as a school of sick fish, we are." Her red cap still sat crookedly on her head. "Hurry!"

Jingle dug in his heels. "The Captain," he whispered. Then his voice shot up high. "What if she turns me into a rock or a bird?"

Sander growled impatiently. "You know The Captain can't get you unless you're in her waters."

"Or her tunnels. And we have to go through those tunnels," Jingle muttered, but he followed Sander and the mermaid into the night.

Becca looked back one last time at the stairway and at Jingle's silver bell. She had a horrible thought. What if she never saw her mother again?

And where were they going with her mermaid?!

❧ *Flowers in the Night* ❧

BECCA followed Jingle and Sander out into the night. The air felt colder here. It smelled of pine trees, just like her living room. Becca tiptoed, chewing on her lower lip. But she felt excitement bubbling inside of her, too. She liked adventures.

Within a dozen steps, Becca could hear water lapping against a shore. Then she heard the crash of a wave. In the moonlight, Becca saw a house built onto a small rocky island near the shore. Jingle and Sander laid the mermaid down on the sand.

"This is it," Jingle whispered to Becca. "The Captain lives here."

"Oh, Great Captain," Sander called. "We beg your help."

"Who asks me a favor?" a voice boomed. Becca saw a figure moving out to the edge of the rock above them. First she could just see the head. Then she saw the robed shoulders. Next she could see all the way to the knees. The figure waved its hand . . . and the rock *moved*. The whole island sailed closer to the shore. Becca gasped. It wasn't a rock! It was a giant ship.

"Isn't it enough that I open the passageway?" the robed figure cried. "Who dares ask for more?"

"Don't you believe her," Jingle hissed over his shoulder. "The Captain doesn't open the passage-way."

The sorceress waved her hand again and a log near the shore turned into a crocodile. Becca cringed, then scrambled backward toward the entrance to the stairway. She would go home, even if she was only six inches tall. Her mother would still love her.

The crocodile came to the edge of the water and snapped at Jingle. He cried out and danced backward, but the big animal didn't come any closer. It just stood there at the edge of the water.

Becca kept creeping away. She tried to imagine

what it would be like being in her own world when she was so small. She would have to climb up her bedpost to go to sleep. At school, she would have to stand on her desk. The teacher would *never* see her when she had her hand in the air. How would she even get to school? The only way would be to ride in one of Adelle's pockets.

Becca started back toward the sorceress. She wasn't going anywhere in Adelle's pockets. Not anywhere! She'd rather be turned into a rock than be six inches tall. The crocodile turned and swam away with a giant splash.

"Great Magical Captain," Sander began again. "Sealily, our only mermaid, is dying."

"Of loneliness!" Jingle whispered out of the side of his mouth to Becca, his voice squeaking.

Sander pointed to the mermaid ornament with both hands, never once taking her eyes off The Captain. "We have brought this mermaid from the other land as a companion for Sealily. Will you make her real for us?"

Becca stared at Sander. That's why they wanted her mermaid! They wanted to make her come alive!

"Who is the child?" the sorceress asked coldly.

Jingle poked Becca in the ribs. He spoke between his closed teeth, "Answer!"

But Becca couldn't. Her tongue seemed stuck to the roof of her mouth.

"She is from the other land," Sander said.

"A child from the other land?! You've brought me back a child?" The Captain screamed with delight. Her horrid laugh echoed around them. Becca shivered. The Captain looked right at her. "Every year I've waited for a child to come through the passageway. Finally, you have come."

The sorceress flicked her fingers. Bright flowers popped into the moonlit sky. "A present . . . for you."

Becca watched amazed as the flowers drifted down toward them. She stood on her tiptoes and reached for a golden one as big as her whole head. The flower glowed with a light of its own. It was beautiful! Then the flower disappeared in a golden puff of smoke. Becca laughed, startled.

"Do you like my magic?" The Captain asked. She didn't sound mean at all.

Becca watched the other flowers hit the ground one by one. A purple blossom disappeared in a purple puff of smoke.

"Would you enjoy living like me?" The Captain opened her arms and pointed all around her at the ship. Her coaxing voice sounded as smooth as a silken slide. Becca took a step toward the robed figure. "Stay with me. Learn to make magic of your own, child."

Child. Becca hated being called a child. It made her remember that she was talking to a sorceress. "Becca! Not 'child.' My name is Rebecca Ladimer!" she snapped. "And I don't want to stay here. I want to go home and be big again."

Jingle gasped. Sander held Becca's arm tightly. The robed figure lifted one hand. Becca got so scared that her knees almost collapsed beneath her. "Please. Please, will . . . will . . . will you make me big again?" she asked nicely.

The edges of the sorceress's mouth moved up into a grin. It was a fake grin. "*You* may have anything." The Captain reached upward and grabbed a handful of moonlight. "You may have anything you desire if you stay with me." The robed figure shaped the moonlight into the form of a girl. The girl wore a long robe and stirred a giant pot. It was her! Becca!

"Learn to use magic," The Captain whispered. "See what you could do!" A row of tiny green circles leaped out of the pot. "Learn to control the wind and the rain." The green circles moved over and fell one by one on Becca's head. Becca couldn't help giggling. Raindrops!

A large black bird settled on The Captain's

shoulder. "Do you want that mermaid alive, girl?"

"Oh, yes!" Becca cried, before she even had a chance to think. She took another step forward. It was as if The Captain drew her in like a magnet. The last raindrop splashed on her nose.

"Then I will make the mermaid real," The Captain's voice grew louder. "But you only have one hour to get her to seawater or she will become an ornament again." She spread her arms wide.

A great burst of wind whipped off the sea and sent Sander and Jingle tumbling away. Becca didn't even feel the wind. She heard the mermaid at her feet groan.

Becca dropped to her knees and clasped her ornament's hand. The hand felt cold, but soft, not like glass at all. Her mermaid *was* alive! Yet she seemed to be in a deep sleep. Becca looked in awe at the ship. The girl made out of moonlight was dancing around the pot now, faster and faster. Maybe it would be fun to learn magic with The Captain. Then she could form shapes out of moon-light . . . like people, or Christmas trees. She could even make things come to life!

The Captain flung her robe back like a cape. She stepped forward to the very edge of the ship. "We will have a contest. You try to get the mermaid to water, and I shall try to stop you. It will be a

way for us to get to know each other." She pointed at Becca. "You will play, won't you?"

Becca felt trapped. She felt as if a net were being dropped over her, a net of beautiful silver threads. But she nodded.

The Captain's voice rose to a singing cry. "Remember, all of you. You only have one hour to get your precious mermaid to seawater." Then she laughed. "Watch for my surprises. There shall be three."

Sander limped out of the darkness and lifted the mermaid's shoulders. Jingle rushed up behind Sander and took the tail. The mermaid's body sagged between them.

"Gently!" Becca whispered. The Captain's laughter echoed around them as they scurried away into the pine trees.

❧ *Lady Mer* ❧

"BECCA, having a contest with the sorceress is as foolish as playing tag with a shark." Sander's clothes were torn and dirty from tumbling over and over. Somehow her cap still sat jauntily on her head.

But Becca pointed at the mermaid. "She's alive, isn't she?" Becca followed Sander and Jingle out of the pine trees. She could still hear the waves crashing on the shore nearby. "This is turning into a real adventure! A sorceress and a live mermaid and a contest."

"That's exactly what The Captain is like, Becca," Sander warned. "She tries to enchant children with her magic. Like she's doing with you." Sander made a disgusted sound. "Raindrops."

"They were fun!" Becca objected.

"Becca, don't you understand?" Jingle cried. "The sorceress needs someone to take her place. To be the new Captain when she gets old." His voice rose higher and higher. "She needs a child. To help her now with her horrid tricks. To make her power greater!"

"She has tried with all the children of Seatown and failed," Sander said. "You are her last chance."

Becca shivered, half in horror and half in excitement. *Me . . . be the new Captain? Stay here forever?* She couldn't imagine turning people into animals and rocks. But making forms out of moonlight . . . that would be wonderful.

"Remember," Sander's voice dropped down eerily. "The sorceress used to be one of us. A girl like you. We think that's why she grants us favors . . . because she remembers. Her name when she was a little girl was Swimmy."

The mermaid's body drooped between Sander and Jingle as they climbed up a small rocky hill. *Swimmy! What a funny name*, Becca thought. That must have meant that she was good at swimming.

"Swimmy was one of our bravest," Sander went on. "The Old Captain called to her. Swimmy said she was just going to learn his magic, only the good magic. Then she would be back. One day Swimmy swam out to visit the Old Captain on his ship. She never came back. Now she's as sneaky as a sea serpent."

"So be—" Jingle hopped so that his bells jangled with each word "—careful . . . of her!"

The mermaid's sagging rump barely missed a rock. Jingle leaned back on the tail to pull the body straight.

"Young man, you're pulling my tail," a raspy voice said.

Jingle stumbled to a stop.

"You really *are* alive!" Becca leaped forward to touch the mermaid again. The scales on the tail felt like fingernails.

"Certainly, I'm alive," the mermaid answered. She harrumphed over and over again to clear her voice. Her lips were the same color as the rest of her face. They were bright red.

Sander motioned to Jingle to lay the mermaid on the ground. "I'm Sander. Bet you feel bumped along like a flat-bottomed barge in high seas. No need to worry. We have something to carry you in." Sander untied the bundle on her back.

Jingle and Becca stood side by side, staring at the mermaid.

"Haven't you two ever heard a mermaid talk before?" the mermaid asked. Her voice sounded gentle, almost like singing. She clasped her red hands under her chin. "Don't most mermaids talk?"

"We did it!" Jingle exclaimed. "Sander, we found Sealily a friend." Jingle suddenly turned a perfect back handspring. His feet just missed Becca's face, and he soared way up in the air before he came down. Jingle danced around Sander, all of his bells jingling.

Becca knelt by the mermaid. She was so excited she could hardly breathe. Every year since she had gotten the mermaid, she had carefully hung the ornament on the Christmas tree in front of a light. That way, the golden glass tail and the red upper body had seemed to glow with an aliveness. Like now.

The mermaid looked into Becca's eyes. "Don't I know you?" she whispered.

Becca grabbed the mermaid's red hand again. Her skin felt soft, not hard like the scales. "You knew me once. My name is Becca." Her mermaid had recognized her! Then Becca laughed. "I don't know if most mermaids talk. You used to hang on my Christmas tree. You were an ornament!"

The mermaid looked startled. Her red eyes grew

wider. Then she laughed, too. The laugh was creaky at first. Then it sailed into a high sweet sound that made Becca feel as if she were standing on the top branch of a tree on a bright sunny day.

"I know *your* names," the mermaid suddenly announced, waving one arm. "But I don't know my own." The laughter went out of her face.

"You have a name," Becca said quickly. "I used to call you Lady Mer. Mer means sea in French, so your name means 'lady of the sea.' "

"Lady Mer," the mermaid whispered. Her red lips moving in that red face still looked odd to Becca.

"It's a good name," Sander said. Becca didn't even know she'd been listening.

"How about Lady Bell?" Jingle said.

Becca ignored him. "I made it up from my last name. Ladimer."

No one responded, not even the mermaid. She was still whispering, "Lady Mer. Lady Mer."

"Get it?" Becca asked. "Ladimer. Ladi-mer. Lady Mer." Still no one answered. "Doesn't any-one. . . ."

"Your carriage awaits, Lady Mer," Jingle said. Becca glared up at him. She didn't want to be interrupted. Jingle set the canvas carrier that Sander

had been unfolding down in front of them. It looked a little like a seat — the kind mothers carry babies in on their backs. Then Jingle pulled a tiny bell out of his pocket with a flourish and tied it to the carrier. Becca sighed, disgusted. Now she would have to listen to one more bell.

Sander lifted the mermaid up by the arms and set her down in the little canvas seat. Lady Mer slithered out of her seat, tail first. "Goodness, I'm not too good at sitting, am I?"

Jingle tugged on the mermaid's arms. She looked almost as awkward as Becca sometimes did. Becca put her hand over her mouth to keep from laughing. "We'll tie you in," Jingle said.

"Tie me in?" The mermaid wrenched her arms free and hooked them over the side of the carrier to hold herself up. "Young man, you certainly will not!" The tip of her tail kept flopping.

Jingle flushed. He swung the carrier up so that Sander could slip her arms into the straps. Then he led the way along the path, almost dancing. Step. Step. Step. Jingle. Jingle. Jingle. "Come on, Purple Flower," he said over his shoulder.

Becca rolled her eyes. "That's not my name." Jingle grinned.

"I feel so dry," Lady Mer exclaimed in a singing

voice. "And I'm itchy!" She started to slip down into her carrier again. "Couldn't someone scratch my tail?"

Lady Mer sounded so mournful. Becca couldn't resist. She helped pull Lady Mer up into a sitting position. Then she scratched the scales with both hands.

"A little higher," the mermaid said. "Oooohh, that feels good. Now down to the left."

Becca scratched harder. She had loved this mermaid ornament all her life, and now Lady Mer was alive. They had to get her to water in time. Already her tail was getting dry. "How far do we have to go to seawater, Sander?" she asked.

"To the bottom of this hill, then through the tunnels." Sander sounded worried when she said the word *tunnels*. "The tunnels go under the sea, so The Captain controls them. Once we're through them and in Seatown, that waterlogged, crabby sorceress won't be able to hurt us."

"*I* don't believe in sorceresses," Lady Mer exclaimed in a haughty voice.

"Neither did I." Becca meant to whisper, but her voice shot up. "The sorceress is the one who made you come alive."

"Have to keep her alive," Jingle muttered.

Lady Mer heard him. "Keep me alive?"

Becca touched the mermaid's arm. "We only have one hour to get you to seawater, or you will turn into an ornament again."

Lady Mer clapped her hands together. "Then run! Run!" She started to slip tail first out of the carrier as they all began to run. The mermaid caught herself by the armpits. Then she gave Becca an embarrassed grin. "Faster! Faster!"

❧ *Pig in Red Shoes* ❧

WITH one hand, Becca held the back of Jingle's shirt. Her other hand brushed against the cold rock. They were in the first tunnel, under the sea. Becca couldn't see anything, not even with her eyes wide open. If she didn't find light soon, she would scream. Shadows on the wall eased the darkness. Yet the shadows looked like creatures, each about to grab her.

Becca saw a point of moonlight. Were they at the end of the tunnel? She let go of Jingle's shirt and rushed past him. She found herself in a cave. The cave had an opening in the roof to let in the moonlight. Becca could smell the sea. They must be inside a small island. Imagine that! How many people had ever stood inside an island? She couldn't wait to tell her friends and her mother. Across the cave, Becca could see where the tunnel continued. Water bubbled at the back of the cave.

"Water," Lady Mer whispered. "A swim would feel so wonderful." She arched her back as well as she could and flipped her tail.

The motion sent Sander sprawling to the ground, the mermaid on top of her. Sander looked squished.

"Goodness," Lady Mer said. "I didn't know I could do that."

Sander didn't even try to move. "Rest," she announced.

"Rest? Here?!" Jingle exclaimed. "But The Captain—"

"Just for two flips of a flipper." Sander put her cheek on her folded hands.

Becca was still thinking about the mermaid. Water! She could get Lady Mer some water from the back of the cave. But she needed something to carry it in. Becca yanked Jingle's cap off his head and headed toward the back of the cave where the water was bubbling. Jingle ran after her on his hands. He must think she was playing.

"Thief! Thief!" he called. "Purple Flower is a thief!" He shook one foot in the air, and it jingled.

Even Becca laughed.

"He's graceful as a sail, full of wind." Sander said. "Jingle, you'll have to change your name if you want to be an acrobat."

"Will not," Jingle answered. "I'll just wear my bells."

Becca leaned over to scoop up some water with his cap. Suddenly Jingle thumped his feet back down to the ground. "No!" He grabbed her wrist just before she touched the water.

Becca pulled angrily away.

"It's The Captain's water, Becca," Jingle explained. "If the mermaid touches it, the captain will control her. Remember. . . ."

Becca stumbled back from the water, horrified. If The Captain controlled Lady Mer, then she might eat her.

"The only safe water is in our bay," Jingle said. "In Seatown. That's where Sealily is."

Becca nodded and handed his cap back to him. He flipped the cap high into the air to the top of the cave and then scooted under it. The green cap landed right on his head. That was impossible!

"Sealily?" Lady Mer asked. "Who is Sealily?"

"That's our mermaid," Sander said in a muffled voice. She was trying to sit up. "I've known her since I was a tiny girl. Two years ago the rest of her family was lost . . . to The Captain. She's so lonely. That's why we came to find you. At Becca's —"

"Look!" Jingle interrupted.

Becca twirled and saw him pointing to the back of the cave. Jingle sounded terrified. Was there something dangerous? An animal? All Becca could see was mist rising out of the bubbling water. What was wrong with mist?

Sander and Jingle looked at each other. "The Captain!" they both exclaimed.

Mist spread through the cave. Becca could see it rising around her ankles. The Captain had said that she would try to stop them from getting the mermaid to water. Becca's stomach twisted as if she had a snake crawling inside. So the contest was beginning. This must be the first of The Captain's surprises. The mist rose to Becca's waist. How could it spread so fast?

"I can't see!" Lady Mer cried.

Becca started toward the mermaid. Just then, a bright bubble about the size of her head popped out of the mist. In the bubble sailed a tiny boat.

The front of the boat was a face that *smiled*. Becca slowed down to watch. The boat waved its mast at her.

"We have to hurry!" Sander said. Her head disappeared in the mist. "I'm blind!!"

The mist rose around Becca's face. It was dense like a thick fog, but she could still see.

Another bubble popped up by Lady Mer's head. Inside the bubble lay a lizard with orange wings. The wings glowed. Becca had never seen a lizard with wings before. This time Becca stopped and waved back. She was enchanted.

"Now we'll never get the mermaid to water!" Becca thought she heard Jingle say. The lizard in the bubble flapped its wings and moved over to the boy. Jingle looked dim, as if Becca were seeing him through thick soup. He had his hand up a few inches in front of his face. Jingle wiggled his fingers. He must be blind, too. The lizard sat on his head.

Becca giggled. Sander and Jingle turned toward her. Shock showed on their blind faces.

"There's a lizard sitting on Jingle's head," Becca explained.

"This is not the time to be amused," Lady Mer said fiercely.

The lizard stood on its wings on the boy's head and waved one scrawny foot in the air. Just like Jingle. Becca laughed again. The sorceress couldn't be all bad. She knew what was funny.

Jingle stumbled toward Becca and grabbed her shoulders. "If you can see, help us find the way out of the cave!"

His voice sounded as if he were far, far away. Becca pulled away from him. She wanted to watch the bubbles. And she wanted to think about the sorceress, too. Being able to make bubbles would be as good as being graceful like her sister. Perhaps better. Then she could put Adelle in a bubble if she wanted! Maybe, just maybe, the sorceress would teach her the magic if she promised to visit the ship once a year.

Another bubble with a pink pig inside of it popped up from behind Sander's shoulder. The pig danced in red shoes. It had a red cap sitting crookedly on its head. Becca tried to imagine what Sander would look like as a pig. She burst into giggles.

"Becca!" Jingle shook her.

"Don't you care, girl?" Sander cried. "We *must* get through the rest of the tunnel. Lady Mer will turn back into an ornament."

The mermaid choked. "Dreadfully dark and cold in here," she said weakly.

Becca stopped laughing. She jerked her head aside to keep from looking at the pig. The mermaid *would* turn back into an ornament. Sander was right. How could she have forgotten? Becca stared at Sander and Jingle and Lady Mer's blind faces. They were frightened, really frightened. And she'd been *laughing*.

Quickly, Becca led Jingle through the mist to where Sander was lying with the mermaid on top of her. "Jingle, help me pick her up," Becca said. Together they hoisted Sander to her feet.

Just then, the lizard in the bubble sat on the mermaid's nose. Lady Mer struck out blindly and sent the lizard flying head over heels in a dizzy cartwheel.

The mist was growing even thicker. Becca grabbed the front of Jingle's shirt with one hand. She put her other hand out in front of her so she wouldn't walk into rock. Up above her head, the dancing pig floated by in the mist. After a few steps, Becca's free hand felt rock . . . the wall of the cave! She felt along the wall, moving a step at a time. Then suddenly her hand slipped off the wall into nothingness. "I found it. I found the tunnel!"

Becca stepped into the tunnel and stumbled over a bump in the ground. She fell, almost pulling Jingle down with her. She heard his shirt rip.

"What in suffering seals is wrong now?" Sander said.

"Purple Flower tripped," Jingle answered. "Please get up, Purple Flower."

Becca got back onto her feet and kept walking. Her face felt hot from embarrassment, but no one could see in the darkness of the tunnel. Couldn't she do anything without falling? She saw shadows again.

"I can see!" Jingle exclaimed.

Becca heard his bells start to jingle again. He was skipping! How could he skip down an almost black tunnel? Even Adelle wouldn't do something crazy like that.

Becca rushed out of the tunnel into the cloudy moonlit night. Sander was right behind her.

"The clouds are like galloping horses," Lady Mer said. "Look!" Her voice helped chase away Becca's fear.

"Becca," Sander said. Becca turned reluctantly. She still felt ashamed for having forgotten them all in the tunnel. Jingle was lifting the mermaid off Sander's back. To Becca's surprise, Sander hugged her in her strong arms. "We never would have gotten out of there without you."

But Becca knew she never would have gotten out of there without Sander, either. The sorceress would have won the very first part of the contest.

Becca looked toward the tunnel. The Captain had almost tricked her into giving up her new friends. Becca imagined herself in that black tunnel forever looking at bright bubbles. And she shivered.

❧ *The Black Pit* ❧

LADY Mer's haunting, beautiful singing surrounded them as they trudged along the narrow path. Sander led the way. Becca followed. Her feet hurt from so much walking. Jingle came last, carrying Lady Mer. For once, he wasn't bouncing. The mermaid must be heavy. His bells barely jingled. Lady Mer's soft singing made Becca want to move faster. She had no idea how much time had gone by since they had left the sorceress. Was their hour almost gone?

"How many more tunnels?" Becca wished the whole contest could be over. The Captain was tricky. Then Becca remembered the lizard with wings that had acted like Jingle. She couldn't help grinning.

"Two more tunnels," Sander and Jingle answered at the same time.

"Ttttwwwwwwwwoooooooooooooooo," Lady Mer sang.

Becca and Sander were almost running when they entered the second tunnel. Becca saw Sander disappear into the blackness. Then she heard her scream. Becca dashed forward. There was just enough moonlight in the tunnel for Becca to see Sander clinging to the edge of a drop-off. Becca grabbed Sander's shirt, and pulled her up.

"What's wrong?" Jingle exclaimed.

"Drop-off." Sander panted. "Used to be just a little step."

Becca crawled forward and knelt beside Sander. She peered over the edge of the drop-off. It looked like a deep black hole. Becca lay on her stomach and reached with her hand. Only a few inches down, she felt rock. "I can feel the bottom!" Yet only a moment before, she had seen Sander's whole body hanging off this ledge!

"Magic," Sander muttered.

This time Becca knew. "It must be The Captain.

The second surprise." Becca stared at the black hole beneath her. Why was the magic different for her?

Jingle's bells jingled fiercely. "Horrible Captain!" he shrieked. "Monster! She's playing with us!"

"I don't want to turn back into an ornament," Lady Mer said in a whispery voice.

Becca sat up and swung her feet over the edge of the drop-off. She had to save Lady Mer. She'd beaten The Captain once. The pit looked deep, but she could feel the bottom. Becca stamped on the rock. That must mean she could walk on it. Becca stood up.

"Careful, girl," Sander muttered. Then Becca heard absolute silence, not even the tinkling of Jingle's bells.

The black pit gaped beneath Becca's feet. Ooohhhh. It looked like she was walking on nothing. She made herself take a step forward.

Way down beneath her, Becca saw a figure. A whale formed in the darkness. No . . . it was a dolphin. It glowed softly. The dolphin swam around and around the tunnel. Becca loved dolphins. The sorceress had sent her a dolphin!

"Go!" Jingle wailed. "Keep walking!"

The dolphin swam closer and closer. Becca gasped. There was a boy on its back. Wouldn't it be fun to ride on the back of a dolphin? The boy raised his hand and waved. He smiled.

Becca clenched her fists. No! This was the sorceress's magic. Becca forced herself to close her eyes. Then she shuffled forward. With each step, she tapped her foot in front of her to make sure the ground was still solid. Her knees shook. What if she suddenly fell into the pit? Her stomach felt sick.

Finally, Becca's toe bumped against rock. Becca opened her eyes and reached down to feel the ledge with her hands. "Here is the other side." She stepped out of the pit onto a rock that she could see. Becca looked back. In the light from the opening of the tunnel she could see the others clearly. Lady Mer rested on the ground now. She was rubbing her tail. It must be getting stiff.

"Good girl!" Sander exclaimed.

"But *we* still can't get across the pit, Purple Flower," Jingle said. "And you can't carry the mermaid to water alone."

Becca stomped her foot. She had walked all the way across the pit and Jingle couldn't even think of something nice to say. Couldn't he be more hopeful? Then Becca hesitated. She really could see the ground again. "Wait! Jingle, can you see me?"

He waved one hand and his bells jingled. "Sure."

"Can you see the rock I'm standing on?" she insisted.

"Mighty dark," he said.

"Clear as a porpoise in moonlight!" Sander exclaimed.

Becca took a deep breath and then said, "Can you jump this far?"

"Jump?!" Jingle cried. "But. . . ."

"She is right," Sander answered. "I can see where she is standing. That means the rock is real. The tunnel goes on!" Sander moved back a few feet.

"I'll catch you." Becca stood by the edge and held out both hands. She looked down. The dolphin and the boy had moved closer to her now. Suddenly Becca had an overpowering wish to leap on the dolphin's back and ride away with it into the sea. They would leap in the air together and dive. . . .

Sander jumped so hard that she knocked Becca down.

"Becca! Sander! Are you all right?" Jingle yelled.

Sander helped Becca to her feet and hugged her tightly.

"I'm fine," Becca answered. Sander's hug felt good. It made Becca remember that Sander and Jingle and the mermaid were real. The beautiful dolphin and the wild boy were only made by the sorceress.

Sander pushed her gently away. "Hurry!"

Becca knew what she had to do. She walked back across the pit. She made herself look straight at Jingle. He even held his hands out for her.

Lady Mer had her arms crossed over her chest as if she were asleep.

"Lady Mer," Becca called softly.

"Can't I have some water?" Lady Mer answered. Her voice sounded groggy. "I'm so thirsty. I'm so stiff."

"Soon!" Becca begged. "Oh, please hold on."

"I tied her in," Jingle whispered. "So she won't fall out." He lifted the carrier and helped Becca put her arms through the straps. Becca's knees wobbled, and she almost fell over backward. It was heavy! Jingle caught her. "Can you do it? Oh, Purple Flower. . . ."

Becca took two wobbly steps, then caught her balance. Jingle helped her step down, then let her go. Step. Step. Step. Becca made each move carefully, so she wouldn't lose her balance and fall. But she made the mistake of looking down. The dolphin's nose was right beneath her feet. With a flick of its tail, the dolphin lifted its beautiful head toward her. The boy reached out with his arm.

She could touch them if she tried. The boy was younger than she. His eyes pleaded with her. Becca stopped. She leaned down just a bit closer.

"Becca," Sander said. "Remember, the sorceress is like a jellyfish. Soft and beautiful until she stings." Becca hardly heard her. The dolphin's soft dark eyes seemed to be talking to her. "Be our friend," the boy and dolphin pleaded together. "Please be our friend." Becca knew the dolphin wanted her to stroke its head. The boy wanted her to stay and be his friend forever.

"What a beautiful dolphin," Lady Mer said in a singsong voice. Becca reached back and touched the mermaid's head that rested on her shoulder. Becca just knew that if she knelt down, then both she and the mermaid would be able to swim away. Lady Mer would be real, and she would have two wonderful new friends.

"I feel so strange, Becca." The mermaid's voice got quieter. "Like I'm dreaming."

Becca flinched. She'd almost forgotten *again*. That horrible Captain kept trying to trick her. She wanted her to forget how important it was to hurry.

Becca took another step forward. The boy suddenly stood up on the dolphin's back and reached for her with both hands. If she didn't catch him, he would tumble into the water! He might drown. Becca moved her foot to step past him. "Sander!" she cried. "Sander, talk to me."

"Keep going, girl." Sander's voice sounded so solid. Becca shuffled toward her. "You're going to beat that sorceress!" Sander cried. "I never would have believed it, but you're going to beat her."

Becca bumped her toe into the other side, and Sander grabbed her shoulders. Becca almost started crying with relief when Sander took the mermaid off her back. "Sander, I made it!"

"That you did, girl," Sander said. Her voice was full of pride.

Jingle leaped over the pit like a graceful long-legged bird. He thumped Becca on the back.

They all walked down the tunnel again, Becca first. Only one more part of the contest remained.

Only one more surprise from the sorceress. Becca wanted to look back over her shoulder to see the dolphin and the boy again, but she didn't dare. They didn't have much time. Sander carried the mermaid. The blackness went on even longer than before. Becca cheered when she saw light shimmering in the darkness.

"Oooohhh."

"What was that?" Becca asked.

"Lady Mer." Sander shook the sling. "Lady Mer!" Sander's voice rose higher with each word. "She won't answer!"

Becca leaped back and fumbled in the darkness to feel the mermaid. "Her tail is starting to feel like glass again."

They ran. Becca and Jingle left the tunnel first. A large black bird whooshed down on them. The bird jabbed at Becca's face with its beak.

"Back! Back!" Sander cried. Becca and Jingle dove for the tunnel. Jingle had blood seeping from a wound in his shoulder. Becca wasn't hurt at all. But she was sure the bird had dived at her face.

"Let me see, Jingle." Sander ripped off the sleeve of his shirt and peered at his shoulder. Then she tied the sleeve around his wound. "This will stop the bleeding."

The bird settled on a rock. It looked just like

the bird that had sat on the sorceress's shoulder on the ship. The bird was dripping wet with seawater. "May you drown like a captured turtle!" Sander yelled.

Becca shook her fist. She felt so horrified that she couldn't even speak. Jingle was hurt. The Captain had hurt him!

"We'll never get Lady Mer to water," Jingle wailed. "Now Sealily will surely die!"

✄ *Lady Mer's Golden Tail* ✄

BECCA sat watching the bird as it walked back and forth along the high rock. Sander crouched at Becca's side. Behind them, Jingle's bells were silent.

Becca rocked from her heels to her toes. The bird was The Captain's third and final surprise. Becca crouched and hugged her knees. She couldn't let the sorceress win. She couldn't! She had to try one last time to save Lady Mer. But how?

Then Becca thought about The Captain's magic. She remembered The Captain's gust of wind that had rolled the others over and over, but had not touched her. She remembered the mist that had made the others blind, but not her. She remembered the shallow pit that had been a bottomless hole to Sander and Jingle. And now that bird had dived at both Jingle and her, but only Jingle had been hurt. Becca took a deep breath. She had an idea. "How far is it to the last tunnel?"

"Just past the bird. The lagoon is right there." Sander gripped Becca's elbow.

Jingle moaned. "Half of Lady Mer's tail is glass now. She's turning back into an ornament."

Becca stepped out of the tunnel. "Maybe I can stop the bird."

"Becca, no!" Jingle cried. Becca was glad to know that he cared.

"Let her go," Sander said, but her voice sounded scared.

Becca walked alone toward the bird. It watched her with beady black eyes until she was well away from the tunnel. Then the bird soared high into the air. It clamped its wings to its side and dove. Becca screamed as she watched the bird's beak enter her shoulder. But she didn't feel any pain. "The Captain's magic can't hurt me," she cried. "I was right!"

Becca slowly raised her arms above her head.

Her pajama shirt and her sweater hiked up. She could feel the wind against her bare stomach.

The bird circled and dove again. Becca reached for the bird's foot and missed.

"Slippery as a fish, it'll be," Sander cried. "Grab it tight!"

The third time the bird dove, Becca grabbed one of its legs and held on. The bird raked its wings across her arm and pecked at her wrist. She still didn't feel anything.

"Hurry!" Becca screamed. "Go around me. Now!"

Becca watched Sander and Jingle come toward her. Sander's trousers were so torn and dirty they looked like rags. But her red cap still sat crookedly on her head. Lady Mer hung limply in the carrier. Her head was back. Her mouth was open.

Jingle's face looked ghostly and pale in the moonlight. He had blood on his shoulder and only one sleeve left on his ripped shirt. "Be brave, Purple Flower," he whispered.

Just as Jingle passed, the bird flapped its wings and lunged for Becca's eyes. "No," Becca screeched. She almost let go. Becca closed her eyes tightly and kept her fists clenched. "The bird can't hurt me. The Captain's magic can't hurt me," she

muttered. "I don't want to be a sorceress. I don't want to be a sorceress."

"Safe!" Sander yelled.

Becca let go of the bird. Instead of flying away, it dove for her face. It was too real. Becca crouched down and covered her head with her arms. The bird crowed triumphantly and flew away.

Then Becca ran. The third tunnel was short and lit by a torch. She skidded to a stop at the end of the tunnel. In front of her stretched a bay of water. The bay was ringed on this side by rocks and on the other side by rolling hills. The light from the full moon shone on the surface of the water. There were people here, too. Lots of people. They were all dressed like Sander and Jingle, in trousers and wide-bottomed shirts that came almost to their knees, and flat caps.

"Is she alive?" Becca pushed through the people and ran toward her friends.

Sander and Jingle crouched on the edge of the lagoon. They lowered Lady Mer into the water. Little waves splashed over her body. But the mermaid didn't move.

Neither Sander nor Jingle answered Becca's question. Jingle's face looked terribly sad.

Becca knelt down and grabbed her mermaid's

shoulders. They still felt soft like skin. But they felt cold. Becca remembered everything that she and Sander and Jingle had faced to get the mermaid here. She thought of the blinding mist and the bubbles. She thought of the dolphin and boy that had tempted her to go away with them.

Then Becca remembered taking the red and gold mermaid ornament out of its box every year since she was a little girl. "You have to live now." Becca shook Lady Mer's shoulders.

The mermaid moaned. "You have to live," Becca wailed. She shook the shoulders again as hard as she could.

"Gently," Sander said.

The mermaid opened her eyes. "Becca!" she whispered.

Becca blinked over and over. A lump swelled up in her throat. She felt as if she'd just been given the most wonderful present she'd ever gotten in her whole life.

Lady Mer flipped her tail clumsily. "My tail feels stiff."

Becca reached down to touch the flipper. "The end of your tail is still glass!"

For an instant, Lady Mer hid her face in her red hands. Then she laughed, that same laugh that had made Becca feel as if she were dancing across the treetops. "But the rest of me is alive!"

Jingle cheered. "Lady Mer is alive! Lady Mer is alive!" He waved his cap and shouted to the sky. "Hear that, Captain? She's alive! Becca won your contest!" The rest of the people began to cheer, too.

Sander clapped Becca on the shoulder. "Snagged the pearl out of the oyster that time, didn't we?" She almost knocked Becca into the water.

Jingle bowed to the mermaid. "Welcome to Seatown."

Sander pointed out into the bay. "There's Sealily!"

Becca saw a flash of a tail in the water. She thought it looked green. Lady Mer swam out to meet the other mermaid. Her bright red and gold body glistened in the moonlight.

Jingle rocked back and forth beside Becca. She could hear the tinkle of his bells, but for once they didn't bother her. She knew how much Jingle cared about Lady Mer. Jingle looked at her. "If you hadn't gone out there alone with that bird, we wouldn't have made it to water in time."

The two mermaids swam around each other slowly. Becca wished it were daylight so she could see better. The mermaids leaped into the air to-

gether and dove like dolphins. Then Becca saw the golden tail coming toward her in the water.

Becca knew she had a silly grin on her face. But who would have imagined that she would be watching Lady Mer swim in the middle of the night on Christmas Eve? And that she would win a contest with a sorceress! She was even beginning to really like Jingle.

Becca could see Jingle's toes moving inside his slippers. "You're just like my sister Adelle." She pointed to his feet. "She never stops moving, either. And you're both so graceful . . . Adelle can do anything."

They sat together in silence.

"Is your sister brave like you?" Sander asked.

Becca swirled to look at her. Was she teasing?

"And strong?" Lady Mer asked in her singing voice. "You ran a long way tonight." Becca hadn't even heard the mermaid splash back through the water. Lady Mer stroked Becca's arm with her wet hand.

Becca swallowed, startled. Her sister Adelle never would have even come down the stairs alone at night to look at the Christmas tree. She was afraid of the dark. Becca grinned at Sander and at Lady Mer and then at Jingle. The boy did a backward roll over his good shoulder. He was so much like Adelle.

Adelle could dance and sing beautifully. But Lady Mer was right. She could do some things better. She could run better. And Sander thought she was brave, too. She had been scared when she had walked across that black pit and when she'd grabbed the bird, but she had done it anyway. Becca sighed. Maybe she was special, just as special as Adelle. Only she was special in her own way.

Lady Mer flipped her golden tail and swam back toward Sealily. The two mermaids headed for the giant rock in the middle of the lagoon. They pulled themselves out of the water to sit on the bank. Becca wished she could hear what they were saying.

"Now they will both live," Sander said.

Becca nodded. "Being alive is better than hanging on a tree."

Jingle sighed happily.

"The Elder of Seatown," a voice announced. The whole crowd grew silent.

Sander and Jingle leaped to their feet. "He's our oldest person," Jingle whispered.

"Wiser than all the wiliest whales in the whole sea," Sander added.

Becca stood up slowly. She faced an old man dressed in a tunic of brilliant gold. The skin on his hands and face had more lines than she had ever seen.

The man slowly held out one hand for Sander and one for Jingle. "I see you both succeeded," he said proudly. His voice quivered. "You brought back a mermaid."

Jingle ducked his head and played with the dirt with his toe. Sander pulled Becca forward. "This is a child from the other land. Becca is her name. She. . . ."

"She outwitted the sorceress!" Jingle exclaimed. "Lady Mer wouldn't be alive without her."

Becca blushed. She noticed that The Elder was bowing. To her! "Welcome to Seatown," he said. "A hundred times welcome."

Becca bowed in return. Then she remembered her home and that made her brave enough to speak. "Can you help me get big again?"

The Elder's eyes were green like Sander's. They sparkled. "How did you become small?" he asked.

Becca remembered lying on her stomach under the Christmas tree. "There was this little door on the outside of my tree. I touched the doorknob."

"Then touch the inside doorknob as you leave and you will become big again." The Elder rested his hand on Becca's shoulder.

Becca felt her tiredness drain away. Was The Elder magic, too? "That's all?" Becca exclaimed. "Just touch the inside doorknob?" She could have gone home all along. Becca turned back to look at the lake. But then Lady Mer wouldn't be alive.

"Once before, in my great-grandfather's time, we had a visitor from the other land," The Elder said. "A boy. His name was Alfred."

Becca whirled around to look at him. Alfred? That was her grandfather's name! He had given her the mermaid ornament. And he had lived in the same house when he was a little boy. Had her grandfather come here, too? She'd have to ask him tomorrow night at Christmas dinner.

The Elder smiled at Becca and then spoke softly so only she could hear, "Our sorceress's tricks couldn't hurt you, could they?"

Becca nodded. "How did you know?"

"The Old Captain's magic didn't hurt Alfred, either. The evil only seems to work on those from our own world." The old man tapped Becca on the shoulder. "Now you must hurry, Becca. Dawn will come soon."

Dawn. Becca called one last time to her mermaid. "Lady Mer! Lady Mer!" The mermaid dove into the water and swam toward her. Becca met her at the bank. "I'm going home," Becca said. "I'll miss you."

"Come back to see me, please." The mermaid gave her a soggy hug. "I'll never forget you." Lady Mer swam toward Sealily. Halfway across the bay, she leaped high into the air and then dove straight down. Her golden tail splashed in farewell. Becca knew she would always remember the mermaid just like this.

Becca turned to her friends.

"I'm going with you as far as The Captain's beach," Sander announced.

"Me, too," Jingle said.

The Elder reached over and touched both of them. Jingle shook his body, even his sore shoulder. His bells jingled. Then he did a one-handed handstand. Becca laughed.

"I could outrun one of Lady Mer's galloping clouds," Jingle exclaimed.

Becca stood still for a moment, thinking. Then she hopped up and down. "We'll run faster than racing sea horses!"

"Let's fly like flying fishes!" Sander cried.

❧ Almost a Sorceress ❧

BECCA and Sander and Jingle began the long journey. They passed the tunnels safely. Even the deep hole had disappeared. Not a bit of mist swirled around their ankles. Finally, they crept down toward the beach. Becca could see The Captain's ship.

"We're going with you right to the passage-way," Sander said.

Becca shook her head, though she knew she wanted them to come with her. "No! The Captain might hurt you. You know her magic can't hurt me." Becca looked back and forth between her two friends.

Sander nodded reluctantly. She fixed her red cap so it sat crookedly on her head. Then she looked up at the sky. "Sun will be up soon." Sander grasped both of Becca's hands. "Thank you for the mermaid," she whispered.

Jingle looked at her sadly. "Don't you even look at that sorceress." He pushed her on the shoulder. "Good-bye, Purple Flower."

Becca couldn't bear to say good-bye. But the sky had changed from black to dark blue. She couldn't see all the stars anymore. "Good-bye, Jingle." The tall thin boy did a little dance. All his bells jingled. "Good-bye, Sander." Sander stuck her thumbs in her red waistband. "Take good care of Lady Mer." Becca turned and ran along the path.

Becca ran through the grove of pine trees and in front of The Captain's ship. A bolt of lightning crashed. Becca stumbled, then stopped.

The Captain stood in the middle of the path, her arms above her head. She towered over Becca. Fire leaped off the tips of all ten of her fingers. "Your mermaid lived. Now *you* stay with me!" the sorceress cried. The flame on the tips of her fingers grew longer. It reached down toward Becca. "Believe me, my magic can hurt you!"

Becca's throat clamped in fear. She heard a bird announcing the coming of dawn. If she didn't go now, she would be trapped here for a *year*. Becca looked at the passageway. She could see the mouth of the tunnel slowly closing!

Becca ran. The Captain grabbed for her, but Becca dodged the long fiery fingers. "You can't make me stay!" Becca screamed.

A pit opened up at her feet. Becca stumbled. But the pit wasn't real. Becca caught herself with one hand and kept racing as fast as she could toward the closing rocks. She could still make it home!

A package appeared above her head . . . a brightly wrapped Christmas package with a red ribbon. Becca had never seen such a pretty red. On the side of the package curly green letters spelled. BECCA. The ribbon hung down in front of her. All she had to do was reach up and pull on it. The package would be hers. Becca lifted one hand. Then she screamed in rage. The Captain had almost trapped her again. She didn't want to be a sorceress!

The mouth of the tunnel was open only a few

inches. Becca threw her body into the crack between the rocks. She went flying into the passageway.

Becca could hear The Captain shrieking behind her. She had gotten past the sorceress!

Jingle's bell still hung in the very center of the passageway. Becca reached up to touch the silvery star. Beautiful ringing followed her up the steps. Her side ached, but she kept running. At the top, Becca grabbed the knob and opened the door. She tripped over the last step.

"Umph," Becca moaned as she landed on her stomach. Everything whirled around her.

Becca opened her eyes. She lay on top of a package by the Christmas tree in her own living room. She was big again! Becca looked back at the tree. The little door was gone.

Becca crawled out from under the tree and rose to her feet. She was stiff and sore and tired. Becca slowly climbed up the stairs. Then she took off her sweater and tennis shoes and crawled into bed. She was home again.

✄

❧ Christmas Morning ❧

SOMEONE shook her shoulders. Becca moaned and pulled the covers over her head.

"Becca, wake up," her mother said. "It's Christmas morning."

Becca peered foggily over the edge of the blankets.

"You're always the first one up," her mother said.

Becca's mind cleared. It was Christmas! And she was home. "Mom!" She reached out for a hug. "I went into the Christmas tree last night. Through a little door. The people were only six inches tall." She showed the size with her hands.

"I met another mermaid and The Elder of Sea-town." Becca shivered. "And a sorceress."

Her mother ruffled her hair. "Sounds like you had an exciting dream."

Becca drew away. "It wasn't a dream! It was *real.*"

"Anyway, don't you want to open your stocking?" her mother teased.

Her stocking! Becca jumped out of bed and slipped into her robe. She dashed down the stairs with her robe flowing out behind her.

On the landing, Becca stopped. She stretched onto her tiptoes to look out her favorite window. Snow covered the ground, even the trees. "It's a white Christmas!"

Becca hurried down into the living room. Her stocking hung from a nail on the windowsill. A book and a toothbrush peeked out the top. Becca clutched the stocking to her chest.

Her sister Adelle sat on the floor by the wall, her own stocking in front of her. She sang to herself as she unwrapped a tiny box. Adelle. Her long skinny arms stuck out of the sleeves of her blue robe. She even looked a little like Jingle.

Becca smiled at her sister. "Merry Christmas."

Her sister looked up startled, as if she were

surprised to see Becca being nice. Becca knelt beside her. Did she smile at Adelle that seldom? Her own sister?

Becca touched Adelle's knee. She wanted to say she was glad Adelle was her sister, even if she was maddening sometimes. She wanted to say that now she knew they were both special. But she couldn't find the words. "Wait until you see what I got you for Christmas! I thought of getting you an elephant, but it was too big."

Adelle smiled, a smile that took up her whole face. The toes on both of her feet started wiggling. She hugged Becca quickly across the shoulders. "I do like you, crazy sister."

For the first time in as long as Becca could remember, she felt as if she belonged in the same family as Adelle. She really belonged.

Becca glanced down at her own stocking, but she wasn't ready to open it yet. Had her mother been right? Had she dreamed up Jingle with his bells, and Sander with her crooked red cap? Had she dreamed up the greatest adventure of her life?

Becca turned and looked at the Christmas tree. She smiled. Her favorite mermaid ornament was missing.

⚭